LEON GARFIELD

Fair's Fair

Illustrated by BRIAN HOSKIN

Hodder
Children's
Books

a division of Hodder Headline Limited

Text copyright © 1981 Leon Garfield
Inside illustrations copyright © 1990 Brian Hoskin
Cover illustrations copyright © 2001 Brian Hoskin

Text first published in Great Britain in 1981
by Macdonald & Co (Publishers) Limited
This illustrated edition first published in 1990
by Macdonald Young Books
This edition published in 2001 by Hodder Children's Books

10 9 8 7 6 5 4

A Catalogue record for this book is available from the British Library

ISBN 0 340 79522 0

Printed by Wing King Tong, Hong Kong

Hodder Children's Books
a division of Hodder Headline Limited
338 Euston Road, London NW1 3BH

Jackson was thin, small and ugly, and stank like a drain. He got his living by running errands, holding horses, and doing a bit of scrubbing on the side.

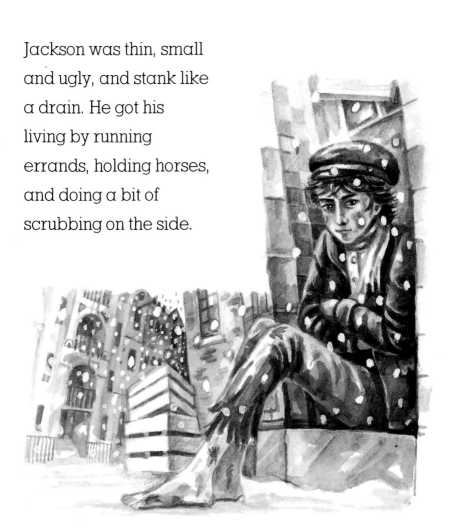

And when he had nothing better to do he always sat on the same doorstep at the back of Paddy's Goose, which was at the worst end of the worst street in the worst part of the town.

He was called Jackson, because his father might have been a sailor, Jack being a fond name for a sailor in the streets round Paddy's Goose; but nobody knew for sure. He had no mother, either, so there was none who would have missed him if he'd fallen down a hole in the road. And nobody *did* miss him when he vanished one day and was never seen or heard of again.

It happened when Christmas was coming on – about a week before. Dreadful weather, as hard and bitter as a quarrel. Dreadful weather, with snow flakes fighting in the wind and milk freezing in the pail.

Jackson was out in it, sitting on his doorstep with his hands cupped together just over his knees. There was a whisker of steam coming up from his mouth and another from between his hands. It wasn't his soul going up to heaven, it was a hot pie from a shop round the corner where he'd been scrubbing the kitchen since before it was light.

He couldn't make up his mind whether it was better to be warm outside or in. He couldn't make up his mind whether it would be better to keep the pie and warm his hands, or to eat it and warm his insides. So there he was, thinking hard, with his face screwed up like a piece of dirty paper, when the black dog came.

Huge: as big as a donkey, nearly, with eyes like
street lamps and jaws like an oven door. Down the
street it padded, with a glare to the right and a
glare to the left, and a savage twitch of its great
black nose. Somebody opened a window and threw
a bucket of dirty water down; and the black dog
snarled with rage. Up it came to the doorstep where
Jackson sat and steamed. It glared and growled
while the snow flakes fried on its nose.

"Shove off!" wails Jackson, hiding his pie and shaking in his shoes – or, rather, in his feet as he had no shoes worth mentioning. "I got no food and I'm only skin and bone myself so I'll taste as sour as leaves!"

"Liar!" says the dog; not in words but with its terrible eyes and rattling teeth.

"I'm froze and hungry!" wails Jackson, wishing he'd eaten the pie.

"And *I'm* froze and hungry!" says the dog; not in words but with its lean sides and smoking breath.

"All right," says Jackson, seeing there's no help for it. "Fair's fair. Half for you and half for me." And he breaks the pie and the dog swallows down half with a fearful guzzle and growl. "Fair's fair," says Jackson; and eats what's left. "Now shove off!"

But the black dog just stands, and bangs at the falling snow with its tail. Then, big as the night, with its street-lamp eyes, it comes straight at Jackson; and licks his face. Not because it loves him, but because Jackson smells as much of pie as he does of drains.

"You're spifflicating me!" howls Jackson, and tries to push the monster off. He gets his hands round its tree of a neck and then cries out: "Hullo! You got a collar on! You must belong to somebody. Hullo again! You got something under your collar. What you got? Stone the crows! You got a key!"

Sure enough, it's an iron key, heavy enough to
open a church. Jackson stares at it, stares at the
monstrous dog, stares at the monstrous weather.
Snow coming down in dirty fistfuls and not a soul in
sight. Not a horse to be held, not an errand to be run,
and his knuckles still raw from his last scrubbing.

"Seeing as how," says Jackson to the monster, "I got time on me hands and no business in view, I'll spare you an hour and take you home. All we got to do is to find the door this key will fit. Shouldn't be hard."

So up he gets; and that was the last that was seen of Jackson, and of the black dog down Bluegate way. Nobody knew for sure whether the great black dog had swallowed up Jackson, or Jackson had swallowed up the dog; and the wild white snow swallowed up whichever one of them was left.

"All we got to do," says Jackson, "is to find the right door. Shouldn't be hard," he said, as they went along the hundredth street. "There must be a door somewhere with a hole that'll fit this key."

The doors he tried! Short fat doors with panels all over like a poacher's pockets; tall thin doors with iron studs down the middle, like a bishop's buttons; doors with little windows, doors with fanlights, doors with pillars, doors with porches, doors with horrible knockers and doors with brass letter-boxes that had eyes inside them when you looked through. And gates! Gates with mansions inside, gates with churches inside, gates with prisons inside, gates with graveyards inside and gates with nothing at all inside.

"Fair's fair!" sighed Jackson, as he tramped on, with the key in front of him and the huge black dog behind. "There must be a door somewhere with a hole to fit this key!"

But there wasn't; even though he trudged every street, every lane, every avenue, every square, mews, alley and court. Nothing. And the worst of it was that the snow kept coming down on tiptoe and craftily muffling where he'd been, so he never knew if he'd gone down that street before.

"I'll be an old man,"
groaned Jackson,
"before I'm done; and
you'll be an old dog.
There must be more
houses with more doors
than you and me's got
minutes left to go. So
fair's fair. You take a
turn at it."

"All right," said the
dog; not in words but
with a terrible gape of
its terrible jaws.

Jackson put the key inside and the jaws clamped shut; and the black monster padded away to the north. Jackson went after, and, while the sky grew darker and the town grew whiter, they tramped and tramped in search of a door with a hole to fit the key. At last they came up on top of Hampstead Heath, where ghostly houses twinkled among ghostly trees, and ghostly coaches with tall white hats rolled silently by. The monster began to whine and snarl and growl.

"Fair's fair," said Jackson. "I'm frightened too. But I ain't complaining. I'm tired too. But I ain't sitting down in the snow. Come on with you! There must be a house with a door with a hole that'll fit this key!"

But the dog wouldn't move. It dropped the key and Jackson had to pick it up before it vanished into the snow. He looked about him. Hard to tell if they were on a road or a frozen river. Hard to tell if that was a gate and a path or the beginning of a forest.

It was a gate. Jackson went through, and so did
the huge black dog. There was a house among
trees, bulging with chimneys and turrets and
looking like three houses that had climbed on top
of each other. Not a light in it, not a glimmer, not a
twinkle, even. An old dead house with an old dead
door, with an iron letter-box as thin as a miser's
mouth.

Jackson said: "I hope
this ain't the one."
But it was. The key
fitted and turned in
the lock.

  "Fair's fair," said Jackson.
"You go first. You're
bigger than me."

  There was a candle burning on a table
in the hall, and a smell of onions, gravy and
roast beef.

  "Anybody home?" called Jackson, up a grand
staircase that lost itself in shadows.

"Home" came down an echo "Home – home – home!"

"I brung back your dog!"

"Dog – dog – dog!"

"I got to be going now!"

"Now – now – now!"

"Well," said Jackson. "Somebody must be about. Somebody must have lit the candle. Maybe they've fallen asleep."

He began to look, first in one room, then in another, then in another. They were all dark and nobody answered when he called. He went upstairs, and the dog followed after, growling and whining all the way. There was a glimmer of light coming from under a door. Jackson knocked. No answer. He called. No answer. He turned the handle and went inside.

What a room! As long as a street, nearly, and tall
and wide to match! Candles in silver candlesticks,
pictures in gold frames, china plates on a shining
table, roast beef on a sideboard and a roaring fire
in the grate! What a room! And there in a chair big
enough for six, at the head of the table, with knife,
fork and munching mouth, sat a small, thin, dirty,
tattered, angry little girl!

"I brung back your dog," said Jackson,
"miss."

She finished up what she was eating and put
down her knife and fork.

"Not my dog," said she. "Too big, too black and
too hungry for me."

"He had your key," said Jackson, eyeing the roast
beef and watching the gravy. "Under his collar,
miss."

"Not my key," said she. "Key of the house, that's all."

"Not your house then? How did you come here?"

"How did *you* come here?" Jackson told her.

"Same like me," she said. "Day before yesterday, just after dark."

"And you're still here?"

"That's right. It were late when me and the dog came, so I slept in a chair downstairs, big enough for six. In the morning there was eggs, butter, milk and bread left just inside the door. So me and the dog had breakfast; then we had dinner; then we had supper, just like a queen and king. And since then, every time I've nodded off, there's been something left to eat, just inside the door."

Jackson nodded. "Fair's fair," he said. "It must be because you brung back their dog. Mind if I sit down and have a bite?"

"Fair's fair," said the girl. "You brung back the dog, too."

"What's your name?" asked Jackson, sharing some beef with the dog.

"They call me Lillipolly, down Shadwell way. What's yours?"

"They call me Jackson, down Bluegate way."

"I cleaned all the silver and polished the table," said Lillipolly, "so it'll be nice for 'em when they come home."

"Fair's fair," said Jackson. "I'll do the grate and the kitchen floor."

"I wonder," said Lillipolly, "if it's really a dog! I wonder if it's him what does it all the time? I wonder if he changes into something else, like a prince, when I'm not looking, and brings the food and leaves it by the door?"

"Shouldn't think so," said Jackson. "But let's take it in turns to watch and see."

Down the stairs they went and took a candle into
the room where the armchairs were big enough for
six. They settled themselves down and the dog lay in
front of the wide dark fireplace and heaved a
growling sigh. Lillipolly took the first watch;
Jackson took the second, and the dog took the third
as Jackson and Lillipolly were fast asleep.

In the morning, just as Lillipolly had said, milk, butter, eggs and bread were left on a tray inside the door.

"It *must* be him," said Lillipolly, pointing to the dog. "He must have turned into something while we was asleep."

"I don't see," said Jackson, "how he could have turned into anything except another sort of dog."

After breakfast Lillipolly swept the stairs and polished the bannisters while Jackson washed the dishes and fetched the coal. The dog did nothing at all.

"Fair's fair," said Jackson. "He's only a dog after all."

"Do you think," said Lillipolly, "they'll come home for Christmas?"

"Everybody comes home for Christmas," said Jackson. "Or so they say."

But the days went by and nobody came, save a duck, a goose and a roasted chicken, on dishes inside the door; until at last it was Christmas Eve.

"It must be a dream," said Jackson, "and I'll wake up and be on me doorstep again, back of Paddy's Goose. But let's keep on dreaming, and, seeing how things has been, I shouldn't be surprised to find a roast turkey and a plum pudding, twice as big as me head, just inside the door."

But Jackson *was* surprised, because there was
nothing inside the door, not so much as an egg. So
Jackson and Lillipolly went hungry, and the black
dog went outside. Nothing came all that day, save
once when they were upstairs by the fire. Six mince
pies in a silver dish lay steaming on the mat.

"We'll keep 'em hot in front of the fire," said
Jackson, "and eat 'em when it gets dark."

They waited until the sky turned black and they
could see their own faces looking back at them from
the windows, like ghost children in the air.

"Time for pies," said Jackson.

"Look!" said Lillipolly. "Look what's coming through the gate!"

Six small children, smaller even than Jackson and Lillipolly, with lanterns to light their faces, came and stood outside in the freezing snow. Then six small mouths opened, and carols came floating up. Herald Angels, Merry Gentlemen and Good King Wenceslas and all. Then came a knock on the door. Jackson went down and opened it.

"Merry Christmas!" sang the children in the snow.

"Fair's fair!" called Jackson up to Lillipolly. "They're cold and we're warm, so let's give 'em the pies!"

So up he went and came down with Lillipolly and the pies.

"Merry Christmas!" they said to the small singers, and watched them go off munching the hot mince pies. Then they went into the room downstairs, meaning to go to sleep.

Two men were standing there, waiting for them! Two ragged, fearful, old and wild-looking men! Two men who must have crept in while they'd been fetching the pies.

"Where's your father and mother?" growled one in a terrible voice.

"Don't know," said Jackson.

"And never did," said Lillipolly. "What are you doing here?"

"None of your business," growled the other man, and bared his teeth like a hungry wolf.

"There's silver here," said the first.

"And pictures," said the second, "and brass and fine china plates."

"We'll take it all," said the first man, with a greedy snarl.

"Fair's fair," said Jackson. "There's a fire upstairs to get warm by; there's a roof to keep off the snow; and there's chairs down here to sleep in, big enough for six. Ain't that enough?"

"Fair's fair," said Lillipolly. "They'll be coming home for Christmas, and I got everything clean and nice."

"Who's they? Who'll be coming home for Christmas?" asked the first man.

"Them what lives in this house," said Jackson and Lillipolly together.

The two men looked at each other; then the first one clapped his hands.

He took off his ragged coat and underneath was a handsome suit of clothes, with a gold watch chain, and in all likelihood, a gold watch too. The other man did the same and the two fine gentlemen stood before Jackson and Lillipolly, smiling and nodding their heads.

"My name," said the first one, "is Mr Beecham Chambers; and this is my lawyer, Mr Chuter & Ede."

"I'm Jackson," said Jackson. "And she's Lillipolly, who got here before me by two days. We brung back your dog. We'll be going now, if you like."

"You can stay, if you like."

"For Christmas?"

"For ever, if you like."

"Fair's fair. We only brung back your dog."

"Fair's fair," said Mr Beecham Chambers. "You've done much more than that. You see, I'm a lonely old man, so I asked Mr Chuter & Ede if he could find two children, who had no homes, who would come and live with me and be as my own. I asked Mr Chuter & Ede if he could find two children who were kind, who were brave, who were patient, who were honest and who were generous. Mr Chuter & Ede said it was impossible. Two such children could never be found. But he was wrong. *I* found them with the help of Growler, my dog."

"How come?" asked Jackson and Lillipolly together.

Mr Beecham Chambers smiled. "Both of you," he said, "must have been kind to have fed Growler; both of you must have been brave to have taken his key. Both of you must have been patient to have found this house; both of you must have been honest for you've stayed and stolen nothing away; and both of you must have been generous to have given away your last six pies."

"There now, Mr Chuter & Ede," said Mr Beecham Chambers to his lawyer, "have I not done the impossible? Have I not found, with the help of Growler, the two very children I dreamed of?"

"You have indeed," said Mr Chuter & Ede. "But they are two in a million, I can tell you. Or even in ten million, I shouldn't be surprised."

"Fair's fair," said Jackson, with his arm round Lillipolly to make sure that he was awake. "Anybody would have done the same!"

So that's what really happened to Jackson, and to Lillipolly as well. And you may look as hard and as long as you like round the back of Paddy's Goose and round Shadwell way; and you won't see either of them there again.

Other titles from Hodder Children's Books you may enjoy . . .

Thomas and the Tinners
Written by Jill Paton Walsh
Illustrated by Alan Marks

"We owe you a wish, and we always pay our debts."

The miners' work is hard, so they need their tasty pasties. When Thomas shares his meal with a strange, tiny miner, he is rewarded with a wish. But soon, more come and no pasty is big enough to satisfy them. Thomas regrets his kindness, but then he faces a bigger problem. Can his new friends find the answer?

Look out for another wonderful story set in Cornwall, also by this award-winning team, *Birdy and the Ghosties*.

The Thief's Daughter
Written and illustrated
by Alan Marks

The key was so beautiful . . . It would open something very precious.

Magpie's father tells amazing stories that bring her poor world to life with riches, and teaches her right from wrong. So when she finds the golden key, she tries to find its owner. At first, her discovery brings only trouble. But in the end, the key brings Magpie's family good fortune – and the most amazing story of them all . . .

*These colour story books are short, accessible
novels for newly confident readers*

JOAN AIKEN
Winner of the Guardian Fiction Award
The
SHOEMAKER'S
BOY

Illustrated by ALAN MARKS

ELISABETH BERESFORD
An exciting story of survival in the second World War
LIZZY'S
WAR

Illustrated by JAMES MAYHEW

ELISABETH BERESFORD
The exciting sequel to LIZZY'S WAR
LIZZY
Fights On

Illustrated by JAMES MAYHEW

LEON GARFIELD
Winner of the Whitbread Children's Book Award
Fair's
Fair

Illustrated by BRIAN HOSKIN

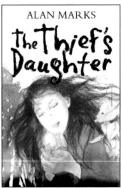

ALAN MARKS
the Thief's
Daughter

MICHAEL MORPURGO
Winner of the Smarties Prize
THE King in
THE FOREST

Illustrated by TONY KERINS

JILL PATON WALSH
By the Smarties prize-winning author of *Thomas and the Tinners*
BIRDY and the
GHOSTIES

Illustrated by ALAN MARKS

JILL PATON WALSH
Winner of the Smarties Prize
THOMAS AND
THE TINNERS

Illustrated by ALAN MARKS